Why the CHICKENS Crossed THE ROAD

BY **Mark D'Arcy**

ILLUSTRATED BY **Jeff Moores**

SCHOLASTIC INC.

New York   Toronto   London   Auckland   Sydney
Mexico City   New Delhi   Hong Kong   Buenos Aires

To Deb, who inspires everything
—M. D.

I dedicate this book to
my silly chickens Charlie & Sam
and my dear wife, Dawn.
—J. M.

ISBN 0-439-84868-7

Text copyright © 2006 by Mark D'Arcy
Illustrations copyright © 2006 by Jeff Moores

All rights reserved. Published by Scholastic Inc. SCHOLASTIC and associated logos are trademarks and/or registered trademarks of Scholastic Inc.

12 11 10 9 8 7 6 5 4 3 2
6 7 8 9 10 11/0

Printed in the U.S.A.
First printing, March 2006

BOOK DESIGN BY
JENNIFER RINALDI

Hector and Harriet were very silly chickens.
In fact, they were so silly, they didn't
even know they were chickens.

"Harriet, I've been thinking, and I think
we might be elephants," said Hector.
"Elephants!" exclaimed Harriet. "How exciting!"

"So...let's drink this water with our long, gray trunks
and then blow it high into the sky," said Hector.
"That's a great idea!" said Harriet.

But it wasn't a great idea, was it?

"Harriet, I've been thinking, and I think
we might be goats," said Hector.
"Goats!" exclaimed Harriet.
"How exciting!"

"So...let's run toward each other really fast
and use our hard, pointy horns to butt heads," said Hector.
"That's a great idea!" exclaimed Harriet.

But it wasn't a great idea, was it?

"Harriet, I've been thinking, and I think
we might be eagles," said Hector.
"Eagles!" exclaimed Harriet. "How exciting!"

"So...let's leap off this cliff and use our big, strong wings to soar through the sky and fly down to the valley below."

"That's a great idea!" said Harriet.

I don't think those chickens are too smart.

Well, they are birdbrains.

But it wasn't a great idea, was it?

"Harriet, I've been thinking, and I think
we might be seals," said Hector.
"Seals!" exclaimed Harriet. "How exciting!"

"So...let's stand up on our tails and bounce these balls on our noses," said Hector.
"That's a great idea!" said Harriet.

But it wasn't a great idea, was it?

"Harriet, I've been thinking, and I think
we might be fish," said Hector.
"Fish!" exclaimed Harriet. "How exciting!"

"So...let's leap into the river
and use our gills to breathe underwater
and our fins to swim around the rocks," said Hector.
"That's a great idea!" said Harriet.

But it wasn't a great idea, was it?

Just then, a little girl walked
up to Hector and Harriet.
"Hello there, little girl," they said.
"Hello there, CHICKENS," said the little girl.
"I'm Isabelle."

"Hector, I've been thinking, and I think
we might be chickens!" exclaimed Harriet.
"Chickens!" said Hector. "How exciting!"

"So...let's use our two chicken legs
and our two chicken feet
to CROSS THE ROAD!"
"That's a great idea!" said Hector.

And it was a great idea, wasn't it?

In fact, Hector and Harriet were so happy to be chickens, they had a big party and invited all their new friends.

**They baked cakes. They made shakes.
They even taught everyone to do the Chicken Dance!**

So, maybe Hector and Harriet weren't
very silly chickens after all!